VIRTUE ADVENTURES

BOOK 1

JUSTICE ON THE ACROPOLIS

BY B. B. GALLAGHER

TAN Books
Gastonia, North Carolina

Cover image and interior illustrations by Blueberry Illustrations
www.blueberryillustrations.com

Cover design by Caroline Green

ISBN: 978-1-5051-1728-8

Kindle ISBN: 978-1-5051-1918-3

EPUB ISBN: 978-1-5051-1919-0

Published in the United States by
TAN Books
PO Box 269
Gastonia, NC 28053
www.TANBooks.com
Printed in the United States of America

Dedicated to
CHARLIE, JOHN PAUL,
EVELYN, AND HENRY

CONTENTS

CHAPTER 1

TRAPPED IN TIMEOUT

"Maggie Mary Murphy! You are not to behave this way!"

That was it. Maggie knew this was not good. Her mom had used her *full* name, looking down on her over folded arms. Maggie sat on the family room floor beside her crying eight-year-old brother, Mac, who was holding his arm.

"Did you hit your brother?"

"Yes, she did!" Mac screamed. "Right in the arm! It's broken! It's going to fall off, Mom!"

"No, it's not! And he hit me first!" Maggie quickly defended herself.

Mac limped off whimpering (even though she had hit him in the arm), but as soon as he turned the corner, he stopped crying. Now that Maggie was getting in trouble, he could sit back and watch the show. Maggie wouldn't be surprised if he returned with a bowl of popcorn.

"Mom, Mac stole my book and I chased after him and took it back. Then he punched me right in the chest!"

"And . . ." Mrs. Murphy waited for the rest of her story.

"And . . ." Maggie looked at her toes. "And . . . I hit him back."

"You know you aren't supposed to hit!"

"Yeah—"

"Yeah?" Mrs. Murphy's frown deepened.

"Yes ma'am," Maggie corrected herself. "But he hit me first! This isn't fair!"

"Maybe so, but you have to accept the consequences for your actions, Maggie. I'll be telling your father about this when he gets home from work. He will have something to say about this!" Mrs. Murphy tapped her foot, considering Maggie's punishment. "But for now, you are to clean this mess up and go to bed early tonight. No playing with your friends. No dessert, and no TV!"

"But Mom! This isn't fair!"

"Sometimes life isn't fair. All you can do is be responsible for *your* actions." Mrs. Murphy had lowered her voice, sounding more like she did during class. They were homeschooled, so she was used to being taught by her mom, but being homeschooled also meant she was stuck with her brother all day . . . *every day*.

Maggie peered around her mother and saw Mac flashing a wide grin from the kitchen.

"You little!" Maggie pounced forward like a tiger on the attack, but her mother caught her by the collar.

"That's it! Go to your room . . . now!"

Maggie hung her head as she made her way up each step to her room. She closed the door behind her, fell onto her bed, and gripped her pillow tightly.

Mac is such an annoying little brother. Mom knows that he bothers me on purpose and tries to get me in trouble! Why is he not punished! This isn't fair!

The Murphys lived on Orange Peel Avenue in the small town of Mars outside Pittsburgh, Pennsylvania. Maggie was ten years old and was always getting into trouble. Her dad was a college history professor, and her mom stayed home taking care of them, homeschooling her and her brother and, most recently, disciplining them.

Maggie had pale skin and fire red hair, with faint freckles across her nose and cheekbones. She loved playing sports and was never scared to get dirty or to slide into home base. Oftentimes after dinner, the neighborhood kids would get together for a pickup game of baseball down at the local park.

Maggie learned all about the Bible, and they went to church as a family every Sunday. She had heard that God was all just and so she wondered if he agreed with her punishment. She had always heard that God knows everything and sees everything. So, he certainly had seen what Mac had done to her, right?

"What do you think, God? You saw him, didn't you? Brothers are the worst! You never had one, did you? Lucky! All he does is terrorize me! And the moment I defend myself, I get in trouble! This is not fair!"

Maggie was out of breath. She was so upset by the thought of this injustice, she had to bury her face in her pillow.

Realizing she needed to calm down, she took in three deep breaths and prayed three quick prayers.

"Jesus, I love you. Help me understand how this is fair. Please protect Mac from me when I get out of this room."

Praying calmed her down, as it usually did, and she even laughed a little bit at herself. But her anger was soon replaced by boredom as she found herself staring at the fan going round and round.

Later that evening, she heard the signal from her windowsill. It was her two best friends, Andy and Kelly. They had thrown a few pebbles up to get her attention. She came to the window and saw them on their bikes. Andy had a baseball bat and glove slung over his shoulder.

"Hey Mags!" Andy yelled up to her.

"Hey guys . . ."

By the sound of Maggie's voice, Kelly's expression fell. "What are you in for?" she asked, figuring her friend must've been in timeout.

"I hit Mac, but he started it!" Maggie felt the need to defend herself even to her friends.

"Little brothers . . ." Kelly shook her head.

"Aren't you supposed to be the *big* sister?" Andy asked.

"Yeah, yeah, yeah! I've heard it all before!" Maggie waved him off.

"We're on our way to the field for a game," Kelly said. "I guess you can't join us?"

"Not tonight," Maggie sighed.

"If you commit the crime, you gotta do the time!" Andy yelled, laughing.

Maggie pulled her window shut as her friends pedaled away. She flopped back onto her bed and began watching the fan spin again. She wouldn't be playing baseball tonight, because tonight, she was a prisoner in her own room.

After a while, the sky grew dark outside her window, the stars began to shine, and the moon rose from beyond the horizon. But Maggie didn't notice any of this because she had already drifted off to sleep.

Little did she know, that night, she was in for the adventure of a lifetime.

CHAPTER 2

A SURPRISE VISITOR

The wind blew through Maggie's open window, jarring her awake. She rubbed her eyes as she sat up off her pillow.

That's strange. I thought I closed the window after I talked to Andy and Kelly.

It was too cold to sleep with it open, so she stumbled out of bed and slammed it shut. This time, she locked it. When she turned back to her room, she thought she saw a shadowy figure sitting in her chair. She rubbed her eyes again. Surely, no one was in her room. But when she reopened her eyes, the figure did not go away. She quickly reached for a lamp and twisted the knob. As it came on, it shined on a young boy sitting in her room.

"Ahh!" She grabbed the lamp and held it up, ready to swing. "Who are you? How did you get in here?"

"Whoa, whoa, whoa. Maggie, take it easy!"

The young boy was calm, leaning back in the chair with his feet crossed on her desk. He had messy brown hair and seemed to be the same age as Maggie. But something seemed . . . *different* . . . about him. Maggie couldn't put her finger on it, but there was definitely something strange about him.

"Who are you and . . . and how do you know my name?"

"I'm Mikey." He dropped his feet from the desk and reached his hand out for a handshake. Maggie backed up, still holding tight to the lamp.

"I'm going to scream and my parents are going to come in here!" she threatened. "How did you get in my room?"

"Getting from one spot to the next has never been a problem for me. I can be here . . ." He suddenly vanished. "Or here." Mikey had reappeared right behind Maggie, startling her even more than before. "Oh, and your parents can't hear us. *Trust me.*" Maggie knew he was right. Her mother and father would have already come to check on her if they could hear them. They were both heavy sleepers.

Maggie had only one choice. She would have to attack. She jumped on her bed, lunging toward Mikey and swinging the lamp as hard as she could at his head. But before it could make contact, he vanished again and reappeared across the room. Maggie spun, dropping the lamp and bringing her fists up to fight.

"How did you do that?"

"I will tell you all about it when you calm down. I don't want to get punched like Mac!"

Maggie slowly lowered her fists. "How did you know about that?"

"Maggie, I've watched over you your entire life. I saw you when you hit your brother today; I saw you when you made that game-saving catch on the softball field last year; I even saw you when you snuck that extra candy bar up into your room."

He pulled a drawer out from the desk, revealing a scattered pile of candy bars left over from Halloween.

Maggie's cheeks turned beet red. Mikey chuckled. "Don't worry, I'm not going to tell on you. That's what confession is for, right? So you can tell on yourself."

He spoke to her like an old friend, like someone she could trust, even though she obviously didn't know him before this moment.

"But how?" Maggie asked.

"Ah, see now that I am not in harm's way anymore, allow me to introduce myself. Again, I'm Mikey, your guardian angel. At your service," he added with a bow.

Maggie laughed. "My guardian angel? That's impossible! Angels have wings!"

"Let me guess, they wear long robes and have halos over their heads too? Oh yeah, and the baby angels are naked and play harps on the clouds?"

"Actually, yeah."

"Don't believe all the paintings you've seen. Angels don't even have bodies. I'm just using this one to talk to you. I thought a ten-year-old boy wouldn't seem threatening, but I must have thought wrong."

"You're in my bedroom!" Maggie shouted.

"Good point. I guess the whole appearing to you in the middle of night thing is a little scary. My mistake. Would it help if I looked like this?" Mikey snapped his fingers. His clothes transformed into robes and big wings appeared from his back. He began floating in the room and rays of light came out of him, almost blinding her. She shielded her eyes as he grew brighter and brighter. She knew it now, though; somehow, for some reason, her guardian angel was definitely in her room.

The rays of light dimmed as he lowered himself back to the

ground. His wings vanished into his back and he returned to the appearance of a ten-year-old boy with messy brown hair.

"That's the problem with you humans. Most of you have to see it to believe it. How do you think God feels about that?" Mikey asked, raising his eyebrows.

"Okay, if you're my guardian angel, why are you here?"

"I was sent by God."

"Of course," Maggie said, rolling her eyes. "And why did God send you?"

"Unfortunately, just like humans, we angels aren't too good at understanding why God does what he does either. We just learn to have faith. It's all part of the master plan. I don't know why he gave us this mission. I just know that he wants us to do it."

"Wait . . . did you say *mission*?"

"Mission, yeah. We have to save a philosopher."

"Philosopher?"

"Yes, you pronounce it . . . fil-ah-so-fer."

"Fil-ah-so-fer," Maggie repeated, chewing on the word. "What's a philosopher?"

"You know those wise old guys who think about the mysteries of man, the world, and the heavens? One is in trouble, and we have to go back and save him."

"But I'm in timeout. I can't come out until my mom says it's okay."

"Ah, I see. Honor thy father and thy mother. Very good. But you aren't in timeout anymore. Your timeout ended hours ago when you were asleep."

"I guess that's *technically* true," Maggie noted looking at her clock. "But will this be dangerous?"

"Sure, it will be, but when God tells you to do something, you say 'thy will be done' and you do it."

Maggie knew he was right. She only had one choice: to follow God's call. "Okay, let's go. But where exactly are we going? And how are we getting there?"

"It's easier if I just show you."

Mikey pulled an iron key ring from his pocket, from which dangled twenty or so keys, each a different size and shape.

"What are those?"

"I call them the 'Keys to the Kingdom.' That's a fun a little Bible reference for ya!" Mikey said, winking. "But no, they aren't *those* keys, those ones Jesus gave to Peter. My keys aren't quite that important. I know they don't look like much, but check this out!" Mikey approached her closet door and slipped a key into the lock. He flashed a smile over his shoulder, twisted the key, and opened the door.

Behind the door, two samurai fighting in front of a Japanese palace appeared. They swung their swords at each other, blocking and then striking, but after a moment, the two warriors stopped and faced Mikey and Maggie. They grunted at each other, confused, before charging right at them with their swords raised high while letting out a fierce battle cry! Just before they reached the doorway, Mikey slammed the door in their faces. He pulled the key out, inserted another, and reopened the door again, this time revealing a man painting the ceiling of a chapel.

"Hey, Michelangelo!" Mikey called to the painter. The man dropped his paintbrush, eyes wide and locked on them. He slowly waved in return as Mikey closed the door again. "I always wanted to meet him."

He inserted another key, this time revealing an underwater scene, as if the deep blue of the ocean was contained in her closet. Except, somehow, no water came into her room. It was as if the invisible glass wall of an aquarium blocked the water from flooding in. A large blue whale swam by, bellowing a greeting to them. Following the whale came a great white shark, and unlike the whale, it began to swim toward them . . . *fast*.

He flashed his massive teeth as Maggie backed up. "Ah, okay, you can shut the door again!"

Mikey shut it just before the shark reached the opening. Almost thirty seconds went by without a word. Mikey waited, tapping his foot impatiently.

"Maggie? Hellooo?"

Still no response.

"Maggie! God sent your guardian angel to take you back in time to save a philosopher! Are you ready?"

"Umm, yeah, just let me get my shoes." She began looking all over the floor.

"Don't need any!" Mikey hooked her arm and pulled her to the door. "Just trust me."

Mikey searched through his key ring until he found an old stone key. It could have been thousands of years old. He put it through the keyhole, turned the lock, and opened the door. Maggie gasped when she was met by stone pillars and a large paved courtyard.

"Ready to answer his call?" Mikey asked. With all the courage she could muster, Maggie nodded and stepped through the doorway alongside her guardian angel. The door closed behind them and disappeared.

She was now on the "other side," though she was unsure of where she was, or *when* she was for that matter. She felt the warm air blow over her and the light blinded her at first. She stepped forward into the courtyard and gazed up a high hill where a large white-stone building with tall pillars came into view.

"What is that place?" she asked.

"*That* is the Parthenon," Mikey answered. "Welcome to ancient Greece, Maggie."

CHAPTER 3

CHASED ACROSS THE ACROPOLIS

As they ascended the hill leading to the city, Maggie could not believe her eyes as they scanned the different stone buildings and large statues around her. Nothing she had seen in America was like this. Everything was made of smooth stone, spotless marble, and shining bronze. There were no streetlights or cars, only people walking around in funny clothes—tunics and togas—carrying wicker baskets full of food and fabrics.

"This is the city of Athens, and we are standing on the Acropolis," Mikey said. Maggie peered down the hill and saw a market and a collection of houses below.

"The Acropolis?"

"The Acropolis is the center of the city where people sell goods and run the government." Mikey led Maggie farther into the courtyard. "See all these buildings? They are temples to other gods."

"Other gods? I thought there was only *one* God?"

Mikey laughed. "There is. But they don't know that yet! We're in the year 399 BC. What do you think BC stands for? *Before Christ* . . . Jesus hasn't come yet to teach everyone about God. The Greeks worshiped all kinds of gods—gods of the sea, wisdom, the sun, and even war."

"They had a god of war?'"

"Yep, the Greeks fought in a lot of wars."

"But none of these gods are real?"

"That's right. They built these huge temples, all for nothing," Mikey smirked and shrugged.

People in long robes entered and exited the different temples erected for the glory of the gods. Maggie wondered how they could believe that the sea had its own god. But as she stood there considering them, it appeared they were equally considering her. She felt their confused stares all around her and quickly realized she was the one who stood out, wearing her jeans and button-down shirt.

"Hey you!" a voice called out. Maggie spotted two guards approaching.

"Uh-oh! I think maybe we should get out of here?" Maggie asked. But she was now alone. Mikey had vanished. "Mikey?" She looked everywhere, but he was nowhere to be found. She didn't know what else to do, so she bolted.

"Hey! Stop right there!" one of the guards yelled.

Maggie ran through the city gates and up a gray-stoned path. She turned left at a fork and continued up the hill of the Acropolis until she came upon a long building. She ducked inside and ran

through
the shadows of
the temple, only lit by large
torches. She passed a large wooden statue of
a lady holding a bow and arrow and weaved through the
columns lining the inside of the temple. Maggie could hear the
guard's steps echoing close behind her.

A man in long robes shook his fist at her as she zoomed past
him. "Hey! No running in here! This is the temple of Artemis,
goddess of the hunt!"

"It's okay!" Maggie yelled over her shoulder. "She's not real!"

The guards continued their chase as she jumped out of the temple.

"Mikey, where are you?" she asked to the sky. Her legs were beginning to weaken, but she kept running to the largest nearby building—the Parthenon. Inside, she ran by a row of large columns on either side and stopped when she saw a huge golden statue at the end. It was Athena, the goddess of wisdom. Maggie had never seen such a large and beautiful statue before.

As she stood in awe, an arm yanked her behind a column and a hand came over her mouth. She thought it was the guards and quickly pictured herself trapped in a Greek prison for the rest of her life. But it wasn't a guard; it was her guardian angel.

"We better blend in, don't you think?" he whispered.

She nodded. His hand came off her mouth and then he snapped his fingers. Immediately, her outfit changed into a layered tunic with golden fringes, sandals strapped themselves over her feet, and a coral necklace wrapped itself around her neck. Maggie then felt her hair moving on its own, braiding itself around her head and pulling itself up and tight.

"I wish I could do that! It would save me some time before church!"

Mikey's clothes had also changed into a traditional boy's tunic. They now were dressed like other kids in Athens.

Mikey grabbed Maggie's shoulder and spun her in the opposite direction just as the guards came through the Parthenon. "Don't look behind you, and walk slowly," he whispered as the guards passed by. They exited the temple through a side entrance and were met by the sun, shining down on a busy city.

"That was a close one," Maggie said when the coast was clear. "But really, you got to teach me how to do that snapping thing! I'd love to freak Mac out with it!"

"Don't you think we should be focused on the whole 'mission from God' we have on our hands?" Mikey smirked.

"Yeah, yeah. We have to save the philosopher. I remember." She stopped in her tracks as a thought came to her. "Hey! Where did you go back there? You just disappeared!"

"I'm always watching you Maggie, whether you see me or not." Mikey winked at her, causing her to roll her eyes.

Now that they blended in, Maggie and Mikey walked through the city freely. They continued through a loud market of people shouting at them to buy things and quiet temples where people told them to be silent. They passed sculptors pounding a statue out of a large stone block and politicians arguing about taxes.

Maybe this place isn't so different than home after all.

During this tour of Ancient Athens, Maggie said, "In order to save a philosopher, I think I need to know what one is. I still don't know."

"Philosophers were the most important people from this time period," Mikey said. "They studied life and what it meant to be alive. They tried to answer difficult questions about who we are and what we are supposed to do. People don't worship the god of the sea anymore, but they still study what the philosophers said."

They continued walking past a large open theater where people stood on stage shouting lines in a play.

"Oedipus! Oedipus!" one of the actors cried out.

"Mother! Mother! I love you!" another actor responded.

Mikey leaned over to Maggie and whispered, "That's a weird play. Let's keep going."

After a few minutes of walking and taking in the sights, Maggie asked Mikey a question that had been on her mind ever since meeting him.

"So, your name is Mikey . . ."

"That's what they call me!"

"Is that short for Michael?" He nodded. "But Michael is an archangel, and you're just a guardian angel."

"Yeah, yeah, yeah, I know. I'll never be as good as Michael. I'm just a lowly guardian angel who can't live up to his name!" Mikey shook his head. "The thing is, Michael is super nice. I couldn't dislike him even if I wanted to! You'd think that someone who kicked Satan out of heaven would at least be a little cocky, but no, couldn't be nicer!"

Maggie couldn't help but chuckle. He seemed very bothered by the fact that he shared his name with the most powerful angel of all.

"Maybe we could use his help saving the philosopher? Call in a favor!" Maggie suggested, though in truth, she really just wanted to meet St. Michael.

"We got this, Maggie. God asked *us* to do it."

"I guess I'm just stuck with you, huh?" Maggie asked, still chuckling to herself.

"Oh, you want to do this by yourself?" He snapped his fingers and disappeared.

"No! No! Come back! I was just kidding! You're a great guardian angel, Mikey! I couldn't ask for anyone better!"

"That was nice of you to say!" Mikey said, reappearing on the other side of her.

Together they laughed and continued to talk about all kinds of things. Maggie recalled times that she had gotten hurt and asked where he was when she broke her collarbone playing baseball. Mikey explained that God sometimes allows bad things to happen because he can bring some good from them. Maggie rubbed her collarbone and had to admit that her arm was stronger than ever after it healed and that she could throw a much better curveball because of it. But as if to defend himself, Mikey quickly explained all the times he saved her without her even knowing she was in danger. They teased each other and quickly became friends as they continued their tour of Ancient Athens.

"I just realized, I have no idea where we're going," Maggie said.

"Don't worry about it, 'cause we're here!"

They came to another courtyard where an old man sat on a large stone bench. He had a very long beard and a swollen stomach. His wrinkled eyes were closed as if deep in thought.

"Do you know who that is?" Mikey asked.

"No, who?"

"That is Socrates."

"Who?"

"Socrates. He's one of the most famous *philosophers* in the world, and he's in big trouble."

Maggie gasped. *This must be the man I'm supposed to save!*

CHAPTER 4

QUESTIONS FOR SOCRATES

"This is who we are supposed to save?" Maggie asked.

Mikey nodded. "People are saying he is disrespecting the goddess Athena and harming the kids of Athens with his ideas. He's about to go on trial."

"Trial?"

"That's where people decide if he's innocent or guilty. If he's innocent, they will let him go, but if he's guilty, they will decide on his punishment."

"What could his punishment be?"

"The history books tell us that he will be found guilty and put to death."

"Death?" Maggie repeated. "They would kill a philosopher?"

"Yes, they would. Unfortunately, ancient civilizations put a lot of people to death."

"If we know Socrates dies, can I even stop it from happening?"

"I guess there's only one way to find out," Mikey shrugged.

Maggie figured if God wanted her to save this man, there must be a way. She decided that she would do what she could and began marching to Socrates. "I got your back!" Mikey called to her, following a few steps behind.

"You're my guardian angel; you better have my back!"

Mikey chuckled as Maggie continued forward, stopping just a few feet before Socrates.

"Hello," she said, but his eyes remained closed. "Hello?" she said a little louder. Still nothing. "Hello!" she screamed, now shaking his shoulder. Finally, the old man was startled awake.

"Yes . . . what, what is it?" His eyes met Maggie. "Oh . . . hello there."

"Is your name Socrates?"

"Yes, it is. And who exactly are you? And where did you come from?" he asked, looking around, probably for her parents, Maggie thought.

"My name's Maggie, and this is my . . . *friend* . . . Mikey. We aren't from around here. But we heard that you're being put on trial?" she asked, trying to shift the conversation back to him.

"Well, yes, but how did you . . ."

"For what?" she asked.

"The charges against me are for impiety and corrupting the youth."

"What does that mean?"

"It means I am not a good influence on the children of Athens. They don't like what I am teaching."

"What are you teaching them that is so bad?"

"I'm teaching them that they should keep asking questions and always seek to know more. It's difficult, though, because many people like to think they know everything. People also don't like to change. They feel like they are doing everything right and get upset when you correct them."

"How do you know what they are doing is wrong?" she asked.

"I don't. I just challenge them to make sure it is. We know what is right and what is wrong deep inside us, but for some reason, we can't seem to remember it all the time."

"I got in trouble before I came here. How do I know if I actually did something wrong or not?"

"Stop a second and ask yourself," Socrates said, looking down his round nose at her. Her insides fell a little bit as the guilt returned. She knew she shouldn't have treated her mom that way, and although Mac probably deserved to be punched back, she shouldn't have hit him.

"Yes, I guess I did do something wrong."

"And you got in trouble for it?"

Maggie nodded.

"Good! Justice was served then, and justice is the most important virtue!"

"What's a virtue?"

"A virtue is a good habit," Socrates responded.

"So, it was good that I got in trouble?"

"Yes, it was. You sure do ask a lot of questions, Maggie."

"Do you think asking a lot of questions is a good way to learn things?" Maggie asked.

"Yes, indeed, which means it's a good way to teach things as well. That's how I teach my students. I ask questions to help them arrive to wisdom on their own. I must lead them to the answers rather than telling them the answers."

"Does anyone else teach like that?"

"Not that I know of," his hand came to his chin in thought.

"Well you should take credit for it then! Give it a name, maybe something like . . . the Socratic teaching method!"

Socrates considered this for a moment. "That has a nice ring to it actually."

Maggie perked up on a thought. "Say, I'd love to pick your brain some more. I have a lot more questions. Do you have some time to chat?"

Socrates's lips parted into another toothy smile, fascinated by the crazy little girl before him. "Why, of course."

And so, Maggie and Socrates spoke all afternoon about all kinds of things. Maggie wasn't like anyone Socrates had ever met, and Socrates wasn't like anyone Maggie had ever met. Maggie was young, Socrates old. Maggie was a girl, Socrates a man. Maggie played baseball; Socrates had never even heard of baseball. Socrates thought and taught all day, while Maggie tried her best to avoid schoolwork.

But even though they were complete opposites, they very quickly became friends. Socrates loved how Maggie searched for answers to why things are the way they are, and Maggie loved how Socrates always seemed to walk her toward answers that made sense.

"You don't strike me as someone who would 'corrupt the youth.' I've been talking to you all day and you just seem like a sweet old man who wants to understand things better. It seems to me like you *are* innocent and Athens is putting you on trial for something you didn't even do."

"They are. I just teach what I think to be true about virtue. I tell people to examine themselves, for we do not know the full extent of the truth."

Maggie fell silent as her thoughts drifted back to her own situation at home.

"Can I ask you a question, Mr. Socrates?"

"You have asked me many already, but I see no reason why you can't ask another."

"Remember how I told you I got in trouble with my mom? I feel bad about it, but I don't know why. So, this is what happened . . . My little brother Mac stole my book and started running through the house. I chased him because I wanted my book back. Then, when I took it back, he punched me! Me, a girl! He punched me right in the chest! And then I punched him back. My mom was so mad she sent me to my room for the night with no television or dessert, and I couldn't even play with my friends. I told her that it wasn't fair because it wouldn't have happened if Mac had not taken my book and hit me. So, I want to ask you, is it fair that *I* got in trouble even though it was someone else's fault? He really did hit me first!"

Socrates froze with a blank expression. "What is television?"

"Oh, right . . . we're in ancient Greece. Ah . . . television is this little box that you watch, and . . . forget it, it's hard to explain. It's just something kids like and so it was a terrible punishment to have it taken away. Take my word for it."

"Fair enough. But if you punched your brother back, then *you* are responsible, because we are responsible for our reactions, are we not?"

"What do you mean?"

"Sometimes people will do bad things to us," he explained, "but that doesn't mean we can act wrong in return. We are responsible for not only how we act but how we *respond* to how other people act. So even though your little brother stole something from you and hit you, that doesn't give you the right to do the same to him. I think that's why you feel bad, because you know deep down inside that you shouldn't have hit him back."

"I guess you're right," Maggie admitted. "I shouldn't have hit him back and I was really rude to my mom."

"It's okay. If she is like most mothers I know, she loves you very much."

His eyes lifted past her and he let out a long, defeated sigh as two men dressed in the gear of soldiers crested the hill and began approaching.

"Look! There he is again, corrupting the youth!" one of them yelled.

"Who are those guys?" Maggie asked.

"Looks like the soldiers sent out to arrest me and bring me to trial."

The guards pulled their swords from their sheaths. "Take him straight to the Agora!" the second guard ordered. "Call the assembly! He's going on trial today before he brainwashes this little girl like he did the others, filling their heads with his crazy ideas!"

One of the guards grabbed Socrates and slapped iron handcuffs on his wrists.

"You can't do that!" Maggie screamed. "He wasn't corrupting me. He was teaching me about justice! He hasn't done anything wrong!"

The guards ignored Maggie, mumbling something about how Socrates had already brainwashed her.

They began to pull Socrates away, but before he fell out of view, he yelled to Maggie, "It'll be okay, Maggie!"

But somehow, Maggie knew it wouldn't be.

CHAPTER 5

THE PHILOSOPHER ON TRIAL

Maggie and Mikey followed at a distance as the soldiers brought Socrates down the Acropolis. Every so often, they would take cover behind a tree or bush, peeking their heads over to see where the soldiers would turn next. After walking a long network of trails, the soldiers came to the base of the Acropolis. Inside the stone of the cliff on which the Acropolis was perched rested three small caves with iron barred doors.

A ten-foot high gate enclosed the area and a guard stood watch at its entryway. Upon seeing Socrates escorted by the guards, hands cuffed in front of him, the main gate opened, and Socrates was placed in the right most cell. As he entered the cave, the shadow of the cell swallowed him whole and the door was locked behind him.

Maggie and Mikey found a large boulder and crouched behind it surveying the area. Maggie's eyes locked on a ladder left behind by someone who used it to pull fruit down from trees.

She nudged Mikey. "You think we could use that?"

"For what?"

"To jump the wall and break Socrates out!"

"Are you crazy? Don't you get it. Socrates is going on trial. The people of Athens will determine if he is guilty or not."

"But he's not guilty. I saw it in his eyes. He's just trying to form virtue and encourage people to do so as well."

"But you don't get to decide if he is guilty or not. That's not how justice works," Mikey explained.

"So, I have to let the trial happen?"

"What did Socrates say himself? You are responsible for your reactions, even when something doesn't seem fair."

Maggie couldn't help but think of Mac crying and holding his arm after she hit him back.

"But it's *not* fair!"

"That's exactly what you said when your mom sent you to your room," Mikey said, reminding her that he truly was always watching over her.

Maggie plopped down against the boulder, fighting back tears. "Don't you understand? It's my fault. They arrested him because of me. I'm supposed to save a philosopher, not get one in trouble."

"They were planning on arresting him long before you got here, Maggie," Mikey assured her, but it didn't help.

Not much was said between Maggie and Mikey as they wandered aimlessly around the Acropolis waiting for the trial to begin. Maggie reflected on how she could have acted and why bad things are allowed to happen to good people, among other questions she always wanted answered.

Maggie could hear people spreading the news of Socrates's arrest. Word was obviously getting around, and so it didn't surprise Maggie to see hundreds of people gathered at the People's Court. The People's Court was a flat area surrounded by rows of seating in a half moon shape. Each level was slightly higher, as if it were a movie theater back home. A group of about one hundred men were seated together off to the side, while the general public filled the remaining seats.

Mikey leaned over to Maggie, pointing to those sitting off to the side. "That's the jury."

"What is a jury?" she asked.

"When someone is on trial, oftentimes a group of people, instead of a judge, will decide whether they think the person is guilty or not based on the evidence presented. This group of people is called the jury."

"What if they're wrong?"

"Then an innocent man will be punished."

Maggie thought of how Mikey said that Socrates would be found guilty, but she couldn't believe that it would happen—not with how nice and wise he was. Socrates spotted her in the back row and flashed his toothy grin. His hands were cuffed and he was standing before the city waiting to be judged, yet the old man still smiled at his new friend.

"Attention! Attention!" a man called out. A hush came over the crowd. "We are here for the trial of Socrates. He is charged

with impiety and corrupting the youth! Meletus will lay out his accusations now."

Just then, a man with a darker toga stood and took the floor. His nose and chin came to a point as if he was a fox on the hunt. "I bring this man, Socrates, who we all know here, to the jury under the accusations of impiety to our gods and corrupting the youth of Athens! His teachings have instilled doubt in young men's heads, causing them to question every-thing. He does not acknowledge the gods of our city, and he is

introducing new gods to the youth. This can no longer go on, for the very future of Athens is at stake!" Meletus proclaimed, his voice booming off of the walls of the amphitheater.

The jury erupted in discussion.

"He has done no wrong!" someone yelled.

"He brainwashed my son!" another shouted. Maggie realized interrupting the trial to defend Socrates wouldn't make a difference. Who would listen to *her*?

Through all of the commotion, Maggie noticed one man

remaining completely calm. He was sitting on the edge of the crowd at a table. Papers and parchment were laid in front of him and he wrote feverishly everything he was hearing. Maggie turned back to the main floor when Socrates stood for his defense.

"Men of the jury, can you not see that many of the accusations brought against me stem from rumors throughout the city. All I have done is sought understanding and virtue. I have explained that we often think we know everything, yet we do not. So, we must self-reflect and seek the truth. Old men are too set in their ways and do not have the energy nor desire to seek the truth. As such, the youth of Athens have listened and sought the truth as they should. If you call this corrupting the youth, then I am guilty as charged!"

The crowd erupted but quickly silenced as Meletus shot back up from his seat.

"But why is it so important to self-reflect?"

"The unexamined life is not worth living!" Socrates turned to the jury. "One thing only I know, and that is that I know nothing."

Shock swept over the crowd. Maggie too could not believe what he was saying.

What do you mean you know nothing? You're one of the wisest men to ever live!

"Why do you teach if you claim you know nothing?" Meletus pressed.

"Is teaching not simply a pursuit of the truth? Is it not merely an exploration of right and wrong? Men of Athens, I honor and love you, but I shall obey god rather than you, and while I have life and strength, I shall never cease from the practice and teaching of philosophy."

"If you won't stop with this nonsense, then I move for the jury to vote. The punishment should be death!"

At this, Socrates turned to the jury and took a step forward. "The difficulty, my friends, is not in avoiding death, but in avoiding wickedness, for that runs faster than death."

"Socrates, you are a crazy man!" Meletus laughed. "Do you not understand that this jury holds your fate in their hands?"

"We should not think so much of what people will say about us, but what he will say who understands justice and injustice, the One, that is, and the Truth himself," Socrates explained. He then sat down and said no more.

"Amazing . . . he's not afraid to die," Maggie whispered to Mikey. The head of the court called for a vote from the jury and began collecting them. As he did so, Maggie noticed the man recording everything that had been happening. She thought she could see a tear in his eye.

"The verdict is in!" the head of the court yelled. The crowd silenced as he took center stage before the court. "By a margin of thirty votes, this man, Socrates, is found guilty! The penalty for these crimes is death by poison!"

CHAPTER 6

PLATO! NOT PLAY-DOH!

Maggie stood there with Mikey stunned as the People's Court erupted in cheers and cries. Even though Mikey had told her what the verdict was going to be, it didn't make it any easier to watch. Maggie's eyes wandered around the amphitheater as if looking for answers and only stopped when they found the old man who had recorded the trial. He picked up his papers, put them in a bag, and let out a long sigh.

"Who is that?" Maggie asked Mikey.

"That's Plato."

"Play-Doh?" she asked. "Like that sticky stuff Mac plays with?"

"Not Play-Doh! Play-*toe*. He's a young philosopher and a close friend of Socrates."

Maggie studied the man. His beard and hair were both wavy, and he held a stern expression that only grew graver as he tried to come to grips with the verdict. Maggie decided she needed to talk with him, so she walked right up to him and tugged on his toga.

"Play-Doh." Mikey caught up and elbowed her in the side. "I mean, Play-*toe*!"

He looked down his round nose at the two young children standing before him, who somehow knew his name.

"I'm Maggie Murphy. I'm a friend of Socrates."

Plato's face hardened. "What do you want?"

"Um . . . well, I was hoping to read what you had written down during his trial."

"Didn't you hear the trial?" his voice boomed in frustration and impatience.

"Yes, I did, but I didn't understand everything he was saying. He spoke of the One, Truth himself. It sounded like he was talking about God—"

"Leave me alone little girl! I have matters to attend to." Plato cut her off, turned his chin up in the air, and walked off, leaving Maggie and Mikey behind.

"He's a little sour," Maggie said.

"I think Socrates was talking about Athena during the trial," Mikey said, "but who knows? Maybe he did come to believe in the one, true God. If he didn't, he must have gotten pretty close, which is pretty impressive for someone before Jesus. And as for Plato? His friend was just sentenced to death, so maybe you caught him at a bad time."

"But he can help. We don't have to just roll over and accept it when an injustice is done." Maggie stormed after Plato.

"Hey!" she yelled after him, Mikey trailing behind her. "We can do something about this! Socrates is a good man. We don't have to just accept this if we know it's wrong."

Plato didn't answer but kept walking, eyes ahead.

"I'm talking to you, Mister," Maggie persisted. But it didn't matter. No matter what she said, Plato was uninterested in the nagging girl behind him and remained deep in thought as they traveled deeper into the city. "You think I'm just going to give up? I think not! I know that what has been done is wrong. And I know that we can take matters into our own hands. And I even know how to get him out of jail!"

"You don't know anything," Plato finally said, whipping around to face her.

"I know a lot more than you!" Maggie replied. Mikey shook his head.

"Oh, really?"

"Yeah!" Maggie proceeded to explain all of her beliefs to Plato—that there was one God and his Son would come down from heaven to die for our sins. She told him that there were three persons in one God and all the gods they worshipped were made up. She told him many things that he couldn't understand yet, but nonetheless, Plato listened quietly. After she was done, he calmly asked a follow up.

"So, is your God all just or all merciful?"

"Both, actually!"

"That's impossible."

"Whatever you say, but there is a lot that is 'impossible' when it comes to God. For instance, when he became man and died for our sins, he was resurrected from the dead three days later. Impossible, isn't it? But I promise you, it happens in about four hundred years!"

"But it doesn't make any sense," Plato objected.

"It doesn't have to make sense to be real," Maggie answered. "None of this makes sense! I'm in Greece, not my bedroom, Socrates is being put to death, and the famed philosopher Plato is taking religion lessons from a ten-year-old girl! It doesn't make any sense, but it's happening!" Plato fell quiet, struck by the wisdom of the young girl. Mikey beamed with pride and gave her a thumbs up.

Plato wanted to forget everything Maggie had said, but something

about her had struck him. He kept looking down at her with one eyebrow arched, as if considering everything she had said. Maggie realized that Plato didn't like her very much, but she didn't care. She had a mission from God and there was no way she was going to let Socrates be put to death!

When they arrived at Plato's house, they discovered that some of Socrates's friends had already gathered there. The room

was somber and only lit by a few candles. Twenty or so men were talking quietly to each other and sipping on wine. After greeting his friends and pouring himself a cup from the pitcher, Plato sat and reviewed his notes from the trial. The top of the parchment was entitled *The Apology*.

Plato read over his notes, deep in thought, while Maggie scanned the room. She could see how upset everyone was. She thought of how unfair it was that Socrates was going to be executed. She wondered why no one was doing anything about it. She couldn't be quiet any longer.

"This is not just! Socrates taught me about justice before he was arrested, and he said it was the most important virtue. This is not justice! Are we going to just sit in this room and wait until our friend is put to death? We can't stand for this! We have to do something!"

Plato slammed the table with his hand, bringing a hush over the room. "What do you suggest we do?"

Maggie looked at Plato, his lip quivered with anger, but she didn't flinch. She stared straight into his eyes and answered through clenched teeth.

"You may be a man of thought. But I'm a girl of action. I know where they are keeping him and I know how to get inside."

She paused a second and glanced over at Mikey. He nodded, giving her the confidence she needed to raise her voice to the room, eager to take justice into her own hands. "I'm going to break him out of jail!"

CHAPTER 7

JAIL BREAK!

"Break him out?" Plato shook his head. "That's foolish! The prison is heavily guarded. You'll never get in, and even if you did, Socrates would never leave."

"How do you know?" Maggie asked.

"Because I know Socrates. I've known him for twenty years! How long have you known him for? Twenty minutes? He has already accepted his fate."

"You don't know that for sure. I'm going to go see him tonight and let him decide for himself! Who's with me?" Maggie turned to the others in the room. At first, there were no takers. But a man in the corner seemed like he wanted to speak up. "You . . . what's your name?"

"Me? Um, I'm Crito."

"Crito! Do you want to stand for justice? Or stay here and cry in your wine?"

Crito scratched his neck nervously as a struggle brewed inside him. Maggie could tell he wanted to help and prayed his courage would rise to the occasion.

Suddenly, a light switched on in his eyes. "Okay, let's do it!" he said, rising to his feet.

Maggie clapped her hands and pumped her fist. "Yes! That's what I'm talking about, Crito!"

Five minutes later, Maggie, Mikey, and Crito were walking the road back to the Acropolis under the cover of darkness. Mikey leaned in toward Maggie and whispered, "You have no idea what you're doing, do you?"

"I'm taking *justice* into my own hands by saving the philosopher," Maggie replied confidently. "That's what God wants me to do!"

"You know sometimes you make it so hard to protect you, Maggie. A jailbreak, really? How much danger can you put yourself in?"

Despite her confident exterior, Maggie's gut twisted into knots. *Am I really about to do this? Break someone that I just met today out of jail? What if they capture me and I spend the rest of my life here? But this is the right thing to do. This is just! And God gave me this order and so I have to answer his calling!*

"Maggie, are you okay?" Crito asked.

She tilted her chin up and pushed her shoulders back. "Yeah! I'm fine. I just think we could use some different clothes, ya know, us being on a covert mission and all." Her eyes moved past Crito and locked on Mikey. Mikey rolled his eyes and snapped his fingers. Maggie's dress immediately turned into a dark hooded cloak. Crito looked back at her with complete surprise. "How did . . . wait a second . . ." And then he discovered that he too was wearing a black cloak. "By the trident of Poseidon, how did that happen?"

Maggie patted him on the shoulder. "You didn't see me slip it on you? Well, it is dark out here. Okay, stay quiet, we're almost there."

Outside the Agora, they crouched behind the same large boulder Maggie and Mikey had hidden behind earlier that day. They peaked their heads up and over the rock to see the Agora's gate where two guards stood on duty. They each leaned on a long sharp spear and wore brown leather armor and a helmet with a red feathered mohawk running up the crown of it. Beyond that gate were the three jail cells buried into the side of the hill.

"Socrates is in the cell on the right," Maggie whispered to Crito. "Do you see that tree over there?"

Crito craned his head away from the guards and saw a fruit tree near the end of the gate. "Yeah."

"There's a ladder at the base of that tree. It looks too heavy for me. I need you to put that ladder up on the gate so we can climb over. Then we'll work our way along that wall to his cell!"

"Won't the guards see us?" Crito asked.

"That's where you come in, Mikey. We need a distraction."

"Me?" he asked. "Why me?"

"If you get caught, you can just disappear," Maggie said.

"How does he do that?" Crito asked. "Is he just super fast?"

"Ah . . .yeah, he is," Maggie said, covertly glancing at Mikey, who only shrugged.

"Okay, well, make the distraction good," Crito said before running low toward the fruit tree.

"That guy is going to have issues after this," Maggie whispered to Mikey, circling her finger around and around the side of her head.

"Okay, here goes . . ." Mikey snapped his fingers and running shoes replaced his sandals. "Gotta run!" He popped out from behind the boulder and started running past the guards.

"Hey!"

The guards quickly turned toward him, bracing their spears.

"You should know that all of these temples are for worshipping false gods."

The guard's confusion quickly turned to anger. "False gods?" one of them exclaimed.

"Yeah, false gods, as in, made up fairytales. Maybe that's why they are always so mean in your stories!" Mikey started backpedaling, baiting them to follow.

"Mean?" one of the guards said, taking a step forward and gripping his spear tighter.

"Yeah, mean! They're a bunch of bullies. Have you heard the story of Odysseus and everything the gods put him through? Poseidon's feelings got hurt and so he bullied Odysseus for ten years! Your gods act like a bunch of babies!"

"Babies? That's blasphemy!" Mikey saw the rage in their eyes and took off running. The two guards chased after him, leaving the gate unguarded. When the coast was clear, Maggie snuck out from her hiding spot and joined Crito at the ladder that he had just leaned up against the gate.

"Hurry, let's go!" Maggie pulled her hood over her head and climbed the ladder. Crito followed and soon they had dropped down on the other side. They flattened their backs against the wall and sidestepped their way to Socrates's cell.

"Socrates!" Maggie whispered to the old man in the shadowy corner. He slowly came forward into the torchlight. "We've come to break you out of here! Let's go!"

Maggie found a set of keys hanging on the wall. She snatched them and opened his cell, but Socrates did not come out.

"One must not do wrong when one is wronged," he said quietly.

"What do you mean?" Maggie asked.

"Two wrongs do not make a right."

Crito stepped forward. "Socrates, I do not think that what you are doing is just, to give up your life when you can save it."

"Yeah, if you're innocent, we have to get you out of here," Maggie chimed in.

"But if I go with you, I will be doing something wrong to correct a wrong."

"So?" Maggie threw up her arms.

"So, the single most important thing you can learn is that the ends do not justify the means," Socrates explained simply.

"What does that mean?" Crito asked.

"It means that you not only have to try to do good things, you have to do them in a good way." Socrates turned to Maggie. "If you wanted to teach your brother that hitting was wrong, hitting him is not the way to teach him."

"Socrates, are you really staying behind?" Maggie asked, checking behind her for the guards.

"Yes. I will not run from the law. That would not be right. Just because a wrong was done to me, that doesn't mean I can do something wrong in return."

She finally came to an understanding. Plato was right, there was no way Socrates would flee. She heard his voice echo in her head from their first conversation.

We are responsible for our reactions, are we not?

She stepped forward and gave Socrates a hug. "Thank you for everything, Socrates."

"You are welcome, now go! Before they come back," he replied, hugging her in return. They ran back to the main gate and opened it from the inside, just as they heard the quick approach of footsteps.

"Hey!" the two guards had rounded the corner, chasing after Mikey.

Maggie turned to Crito. "Go! Run back to the house and tell them what has happened!"

Crito ran toward the city just as Mikey reached out and snatched Maggie's arm, pulling her into a full sprint up the Acropolis.

"Here we go again!" Maggie yelled.

Maggie ran as fast as she could, but the guards' legs were longer and faster. They were closing in. Maggie and Mikey quickly cut through a temple and then barreled past the large stone columns of the temple's interior. After finding themselves at the center of the Acropolis and seeing everyone around them concerned by their presence, Maggie realized the center of the city was no place to hide. They ducked down an alleyway.

"Lose the cloaks!" Maggie whispered to Mikey over her shoulder. They pulled their cloaks off, threw them away, and slowed to a walk as they turned down another street. Maggie glanced over her shoulder and saw the two guards, spotting them and running to catch up.

"I was never good at blending in!" Maggie yanked Mikey and together they continued to run from the guards, who were in a full sprint again toward them. After they cleared the temples, they began running toward the outskirts of the Acropolis. There weren't any buildings to hide in any longer, just dirt walking paths and twisted trees.

"There is nowhere to run!" one of the guards called to them. Maggie's eyes darted from side to side, trying to find an escape path, but there was nothing but flat paths, and beyond that was a tall cliff, marking the edge of the Acropolis.

"We have nowhere to go! I was just trying to help an innocent man! And now we're dead meat!"

Mikey looked over to Maggie. "Do you trust me?" he asked, reaching out his hand. Maggie nodded, grasping it. Mikey pulled her and started running straight toward the cliff. "Jump on three!"

Maggie had heard many people count to three in her life before doing something, but none quite this scary. Time seemed to slow as they approached the cliff. Mikey's counting sounded long and stretched out like rubber bands . . . *Ooooonnnnnneeee* . . . *Twwwwwoooooo* . . . Then suddenly, three arrived in an instant . . . *Three!* . . . and they were leaping off the edge of the cliff!

CHAPTER 8

FLIGHT TO THE ACADEMY

They were soaring through the air, hand in hand. But then, they began falling, first slowly and then faster and faster. Maggie made the mistake of looking down. She saw that there was nothing underneath them for one hundred feet! Maggie's heart pounded in her chest as a scream came to her lips.

But all of sudden, she felt lighter, as if a weight was lifted from her shoulders. After a second, she realized that they weren't falling any longer; rather, they were moving *up*. Maggie glanced over to Mikey and noticed that wings had sprouted from his back. They began flapping and with each push, they climbed higher and higher.

There was no way to catch them now as they flew off toward the horizon. The guards, panting from the chase, stood amazed back on the cliff. All they could see were two children's shadows flying across the full moon in the sky.

Maggie saw that the ground was now two hundred feet beneath her. Her stomach twisted and she began to panic as her legs dangled with nothing to catch her. She knew that she needed to do what she always did to calm down, so she took three deep breaths and said three quick prayers.

She breathed in and out, in and out, in and out.

"Jesus, I love you. Don't let me fall, don't let me fall, don't let me fall. Help me save the philosopher that you sent me here to save!"

After that, her heartbeat slowed and she was able to breathe again. She was still terrified and gripped Mikey's hand tighter than ever, yet somehow, she had full trust in the miracle she was experiencing. They passed over the city gates and, after a ten-minute flight, made their way to a soft landing in a grove of olive trees.

"That was amazing!" Maggie yelled, collapsing on the grass. She kissed the ground and rolled over, laughing out all the nervous energy she had stored up.

"I only use these in cases of emergency," Mike said, tapping his wings. "Guards chasing us to the end of a hundred-foot cliff seemed like a worthy occasion." His wings slowly folded into his back, leaving Mikey to yet again look like the same messy haired ten-year-old boy he had been before.

Maggie's laughter faded after a minute and she just laid on the ground. Mikey joined her and together they gazed up at the starry sky. She had never seen so many stars in her life. "I feel like all we have done in ancient Greece is run from guards and get a philosopher in trouble."

"Sure seems that way, doesn't it? But I think we've done a lot of good here."

"Good? What are you talking about? We were sent here to save the philosopher, and because of me, Socrates got arrested and sentenced to die!"

"For the last time, that wasn't your fault. That was going to happen anyway. You just didn't believe it. In fact, you made a big difference in Plato's life."

"Plato hated me!"

"No, he didn't. You actually inspired him to open a school," Mikey explained.

"A school?"

"Yeah. It's called the Academy, and in fact, it will one day stand right here in this olive grove."

"Yeah, sureeee," she shook her head.

Mikey sighed. "I've told you before, you humans shouldn't have to see something to believe it, but fine, see for yourself!" He snapped his fingers and the sun darted up in the sky and quickly tumbled over the horizon, over and over and over again. It was as if the days were fast-forwarding. Soon, a few of the olive trees faded away and in their place, stone walls shot up out of the ground, enclosing Maggie and Mikey. In a matter of seconds, they found themselves no longer laying on the grass looking at the stars but laying on marble looking up at the ceiling of a large lecture hall.

Maggie pulled herself to her feet and with wide eyes, scanned her surroundings. There was an old man at the front of the class. He had a familiar face and Maggie needed a few seconds to recognize it.

"Plato?" His beard had grayed and his face wrinkled, but there was no doubt it was him. He was in the midst of teaching a class full of students listening intently from benches throughout the hall. "What year is it now?" she asked Mikey.

"366 BC. Plato is sixty-two years old, now the most popular philosopher in all of Greece."

"Am I supposed to save *him*?" Maggie asked, pointing up to Plato at the front of the lecture hall. Before Mikey could answer, Plato stopped talking, suddenly taking note of the new "students" in the back of the hall. He seemed to recognize them.

"Maggie?" he gasped.

Maggie approached the old man up the classroom aisle, ignoring the fact that he was in the middle of teaching a class.

"How did you get in here?" Plato looked her over a second time. "You look like you haven't aged a day since I saw you all those years ago. How is that possible?"

"You were right," she said, ignoring his questions, because

frankly, trying to explain it to him seemed pretty much impossible. "Socrates didn't want to come with us."

It had been over thirty years since Socrates's death, but Plato remembered that night perfectly. "I knew he wouldn't, because you cannot do something wrong to correct a wrong."

"Yeah, I need to remember that next time my brother punches me," Maggie said.

"That would be wise," Plato replied.

"I still don't understand how so many people could be so mean to such a nice man like Socrates. It just doesn't make sense."

"It doesn't have to make sense to be real," Plato responded.

Maggie couldn't help but realize this was the same thing she had said when she taught Plato about God. She smiled and shook her finger. "Someone very smart must have told you that."

"No, someone very *wise* told me that," Plato replied with a smile through his bushy gray mustache.

It suddenly occurred to Maggie that she had completely interrupted his class. His students were clearly puzzled by her entry into the hall and this conversation she was having with their teacher.

"So, you have a school now?" she asked. "And students?"

"Yes, I've had many of them. In fact, I seemed to have lost one. I was scheduled to have a new student today, but he has not shown up. He was a very promising young man. I was very excited to meet him."

"I'd love to take your class, but I probably wouldn't

understand any of it," Maggie said. "And I should really be getting home."

"I understand completely." But before she could leave, he squatted down and grabbed her hand, locking his eyes on hers. "Thank you, Maggie Murphy, you will never know how much of an impact you've had on me. The way you were dedicated to justice, wanting to save an innocent man. You have quite the courage for such a young girl."

He tousled her hair and stood back up.

"You know . . . a girl's gotta do what a girl's gotta do," she said smiling. She then headed for the door, waving goodbye to Plato as Mikey and her exited the Academy.

Outside, Maggie and Mikey found the shade of an olive tree. "I guess Plato is not so bad after all," she said to Mikey.

"Really?"

It wasn't Mikey who responded, but a voice from the other side of the tree. Maggie peered around the trunk to meet the face of a boy a little older than she was. He had dark red hair and a thin face, framed by a short, thin beard still trying to find its fullness.

"Oh, hello. Ah, yes, really, he's not so bad."

"Good! He's supposed to be my teacher," the boy replied.

"Supposed to be?" Maggie asked.

"Yeah, I was sent here by my uncle to learn at the Academy."

"Why aren't you in there? Plato is teaching right now and expecting you." Maggie figured this must have been the new student Plato was missing.

"I don't want to go to class."

"Why not?"

"I don't think like them. They are always thinking about the heavens, but I like thinking about earth." He plucked a flower and twirled it between his fingers. "Besides, what if I fail?"

"If I know anything about philosophers, it's that they don't think they know everything. So, I am sure they will love your unique perspective on things. Besides, what else would you do?"

"I'm actually thinking of joining the military."

"Why would you do that?" Maggie asked.

"I just don't know what I want to do with my life. I figured the military would give me some purpose," the boy admitted.

"Don't you think you should find some answers about life before you make such a big decision?" Maggie asked.

"That makes sense. But where do I find answers about life?"

Maggie shared a smile with Mikey and then nodded toward the Academy. "I would give Plato's class a try; you may be surprised by what you can learn. You could always join the military later. Who knows? Plato's class may be the start of something really special. I didn't like him at first, but then I realized that he just wants to understand things, and at the end of the day, *I* just want to understand things. I think we all do."

The boy considered Maggie's advice.

"Ah, I don't know. Why should I go and think about life when I could be *doing* something with my life?"

"Because an unexamined life is not worth living," Maggie quoted Socrates, which struck a chord in the teenager.

"I suppose you're right. Maybe I'll give it a try." The boy rose to his feet and started for the Academy, but stopped and turned back to Maggie.

"Thanks a lot . . ."

". . . Maggie."

"Right . . . Maggie. Thanks a lot, Maggie. My name's Aristotle. It was great meeting you."

He then smiled, spun on his heel, and walked into the Academy.

CHAPTER 9

RIGHTING THE WRONGS

After Aristotle entered the Academy, Maggie's mind wandered to everything she had seen and done in Greece. She thought about fairness and how it didn't matter if Mac hit her first; she still had a responsibility to act appropriately. She thought about virtues and wondered how many of those good habits she needed in her life. She recalled how two wrongs do not make a right. She remembered Socrates telling her from his jail cell that it is not just important what you try to do but how you do it. She sighed and slumped her shoulders.

"Are you okay there, Maggie?" Mikey asked, looking on from afar.

"I'm starting to miss home, like, even Mac, believe it or not. I feel bad about how I treated my mom and I feel bad about punching my brother."

"I can take you home now if you're ready."

"Really? But I wasn't able to save the philosopher."

"Yes, you were," Mikey said, drawing Maggie's eyes.

"What do you mean? Socrates is dead, and I didn't do anything to help Plato."

"They weren't the philosopher . . . he was," Mikey nodded toward the Academy door, where Aristotle had entered.

"Huh? He's just a teenager."

"True, but if that *teenager* went into the military, he would have died four years from now in the Battle of Mantinea. You convincing him to go into the Academy saved his life. Aristotle is going to learn from Plato and become the greatest philosopher in the world, and it all started here under this olive tree with a crazy little girl from Mars."

"Aristotle was the philosopher I was supposed to save?"

"That's right."

"Why didn't you just bring me here in the first place?"

"Think about it: you convinced Aristotle to go by having an appreciation for Plato. And you couldn't have had an appreciation for Plato without having an appreciation for Socrates. If we hadn't started by going to visit Socrates, you couldn't have saved Aristotle."

"But I didn't even mean to."

"Sometimes the greatest impact you have on people is just by being the good person that you are. It's all part of God's plan, and he has a lot more in store for you, Maggie. This won't be your last adventure."

"It won't?"

"No way! This is just the beginning, but I think this is

good for now. You needed a lesson in justice, and you sure got it!"

"Yes, I did!" Maggie agreed. "Life isn't fair, but you always have to act with virtue."

"Are you ready to go home?" Mikey asked.

Maggie stood up, relieved that she had accomplished their mission. She looked toward the Academy, then back to Mikey. "Yes, I'm ready."

Mikey led her to the front door of the Academy and pulled out his ring of keys. He found one and inserted it into the keyhole, opening the door and revealing Maggie's bedroom on the other side. She started toward the doorway but noticed that Mikey was staying behind. "Are you not coming with me?" she asked.

He smiled. "Sort of. I'll always be with you, but this doorway is your way back home, not mine. I have somewhere else to be." Mikey pointed to the sky.

She smiled and nodded. "Thanks for everything, Mikey." She leaned in and gave him a hug. "Goodbye, friend," she sighed into his ear.

"Goodbye to you," he returned. "Until next time . . ." He held out his hand, motioning her toward the door. Maggie walked through, stepping back onto the carpet of her bedroom floor. She felt the breeze of her ceiling fan and could smell her dirty laundry. Mikey closed the door behind her, leaving no trace of Ancient Greece. Maggie peered around her room, enjoying the familiar and cozy surroundings. Through the window, the sun was slowly rising on a new day.

Maggie stormed downstairs to find her brother and father sitting at the kitchen table. Mac was pouring syrup on his pancakes while Mrs. Murphy was flipping a few more in the pan by the stove.

"Mom! Dad! Mac!" She ran to her mom and gave her a hug before darting over to kiss her dad on the cheek. She even went to hug her little brother, which at first seemed a little strange, but Maggie didn't care. She was too excited to see her family!

"You guys will never believe where I went last night: Ancient Greece! And I met a man named Socrates and then Plato and then Aristotle, although, Aristotle was just a teenager when I met him. And there were these big temples and guards who were chasing us—"

"Who is us?" Mac interrupted.

"Me and my guardian angel, Mikey. He flew us out of the city! He is so cool, and flying is so much fun once you get the hang of it of course."

"And why did you go there?" her dad asked, glancing over to Maggie's mother with a smirk.

"We had a mission from God. We had to save a philosopher and we ended up saving Aristotle without even meaning to! He was thinking about going into the military instead of going to Plato's Academy. I told him that Plato was a pretty good guy, so he decided to give it a try!"

Mrs. Murphy sipped her coffee, trying to gather the energy to digest this story.

"Wow," Mr. Murphy said, folding his arms and scratching his chin. "That sounds like a pretty wild dream."

"It wasn't a dream," Maggie objected. "It really happened!"

"I had a dream that felt real last night," Mac chimed in. "I was on a flying pirate ship and we shot down a dragon!"

Maggie soon realized her family would never believe her, but that was okay, because she knew what was true. She also knew what she had left to do. She walked over to her mother, still flipping pancakes by the stove, and tugged on her apron. "Mom?"

Mrs. Murphy bent over, looking Maggie in the eye with all the love in the world.

"Yes, my dear."

"I'm sorry for how I reacted yesterday. I shouldn't have hit Mac and I shouldn't have had a bad attitude with you. I love you and I'll try to be better, because it's not okay to answer a wrong with a wrong."

Mrs. Murphy shot a confused and surprised glance to her husband. "It's okay, sweetheart," she said, stroking her daughter's hair.

Maggie put her hand on Mac's shoulder. "And I apologize to you too. Even though you shouldn't have hit me, it doesn't make it right for me to hit back. I'm older and should have controlled myself."

"I forgive you," Mac mumbled under his breath, embarrassed by the whole ordeal.

"That was very nice of you, Maggie," her father said. "Let's try to be better next time." Mr. Murphy brought his girl in for a big hug, and as he pulled her in, he whispered, "*I believe you*." When they pulled apart, Mr. Murphy winked.

Maggie knew that she was loved by an amazing family. And even though she got in trouble sometimes, she was getting better and was trying to be good for them and for God. She knew now that Mikey was always watching over her and couldn't help but wonder what adventure he would take her on next time. But for now, Maggie was happy because she was home.

GLOSSARY

TERMS

BC – BC stands for "Before Christ." The events of Ancient Greece happened *before Christ* came. We currently live in AD or *Anno Domini*, which is a Latin phrase that means "the year of our Lord."

Column – A column is a tall pillar used to hold up a building.

Jury – A group of people who listen to a trial to determine if the person being accused of a crime is guilty or not. Juries are still used today in courts.

Justice – Many philosophers argued about the true meaning of justice. Christianity has defined it as giving what is fair to someone.

Virtue – A virtue is a good habit and something that we should try to live by. Justice is one of the main virtues of Christianity.

Philosopher – A person who seeks wisdom by thinking about life. Philosophers study the meaning of life, write books on it, and teach students.

PEOPLE

Aristotle – (384 BC – 322 BC) is known as the best philosopher of Ancient Greece. He tutored Alexander the Great and wrote a great deal on subjects like what is right and wrong (ethics), friendship, politics, and the poetry.

Socrates – (470 BC – 399 BC) is considered one of the founders of western philosophy. He taught by asking a lot of questions, which led people to the right answer. This method is called the Socratic Method. He was put to death for corrupting the youth and criticizing the city. He attempted to improve Athens' sense of justice and was wrongfully put to death for it.

Plato – (428 BC – 348 BC) was a student of Socrates and a teacher of Aristotle's. He founded the Academy, where he and others taught philosophy in an effort to pursue and spread the truth.

PLACES

The Academy – was a school founded by Plato outside of the city walls of Athens. Aristotle learned here and Plato taught here. The Academy is where philosophers met to try to solve problems and understand things better.

Acropolis – was an ancient place atop a rocky outcrop above the city of Athens. This is where temples were built for the gods that the Greeks worshipped. Many of the temples still stand there today, like the Parthenon.

Agora – was the civic center of Athens where the trial of Socrates happened. An agora was a gathering place for people of the city.

Athens – is the capital and largest city of Greece. It is still standing today, but in Ancient Greece, Athens was the "cradle of Western civilization."

The Parthenon – is a former temple dedicated to the Greek goddess Athena. This temple stood atop the acropolis and still stands today as a landmark of the past.

B. B. GALLAGHER lives in a small town just outside of
Charlotte, NC with his wife, four kids and lazy dog. *Justice on
the Acropolis* is his 6th book, but first early chapter book. It is
the first book of the *Virtue Adventures* series.

His first series, *Project Sparta*, ranked #1 in spy thrillers
on Amazon Kindle. He works in Finance for TAN Books and
writes for Forbes.com. B. B. enjoys playing Legos with his kids
and doesn't enjoy watching the Pittsburgh Pirates lose baseball
games, which they always seem to do.

B. B. thinks that all kids should use their imagination, obey
their parents and go to church. He hopes that his kids grow in
virtue just as Maggie does, but if they go back in time to do so,
he wishes that they would tell him so that he could tag along
for the adventure.